"The true sign of intelligence is not
knowledge but imagination."
—Albert Einstein

To Amelia Swan and Margo Moon—your
imagination always fascinates me!!!
You always remind me to see with new eyes!
—Lovie

Pete the Cat's Groovy Imagination
Text copyright © 2021 by Kimberly and James Dean
Illustrations copyright © 2021 by James Dean
Pete the Cat is a registered trademark of Pete the Cat, LLC.
All rights reserved. Printed in the United States of America.
No part of this book may be used or reproduced in any manner whatsoever without
written permission except in the case of brief quotations embodied in critical articles and reviews.
For information address HarperCollins Children's Books, a division of HarperCollins Publishers,
195 Broadway, New York, NY 10007.
www.harpercollinschildrens.com
ISBN 978-0-06-297410-5 (trade bdg.) — ISBN 978-0-06-297411-2 (lib. bdg.)
ISBN 978-0-06-314437-8 (special edition)
The artist used pen and ink with watercolor and acrylic paint on
300lb press paper to create the illustrations for this book.
21 22 23 24 25   PC   10 9 8 7 6 5 4 3 2 1
❖
First Edition

Pete the Cat's
Groovy Imagination

Kimberly
& James Dean

Pete the Cat was happy!
Today would be so much fun.
Chillin' out. Catching vibes.
Sand, surfing, and lots of sun!

But when Pete looked outside,
he got down-in-the-dumps sad.

Dark clouds and pouring rain
could make this good day turn bad.

Pete didn't complain.

He did not feel blue.
Pete knew he could find
something fun to do.

Pete drew a
cool picture.

Pete strummed a
little tune.

Until he saw something too good to be true . . .

Pete found a big box!

He looked it up and down.

He turned it side to side.

And he spun it
all around.

The box was brown and it was strong.
The box was wide and tall.
Maybe this wasn't just any box after all . . .

The box was BIG
and it was GROOVY.
The box could be
something new.

Suddenly Pete's imagination grew and grew and grew ...

Maybe it was more than a box.
Maybe it was more than it seemed.
Pete closed his eyes and had an
out-of-this-world dream.

It WAS more than a box.
It was a groovy rocket ship!
Pete saw the moon on his outer space trip.

10-9-8-7-6-5-4-3-2-1

Pete was heading home.
He landed *SPLASH!* in the sea.

Pete had to think fast.
Now what could this box be?

The box was BIG
and it was GROOVY.
The box could be
something new.

Suddenly Pete's imagination
grew and grew and grew ...

The box was now a
yellow submarine!

Pete dived way down into the sea.
Pete wore his goggles to see the underwater
scene.

The submarine CRASHED! when it reached land.
Now the box was lying sideways in the sand.

But what's a cat to do with a box
that couldn't stand?

The box was BIG
and it was GROOVY.
The box could be
something new.

Suddenly Pete's imagination
grew and grew and grew ...

And pretty soon . . .
The box was not just a box lying on its side!

It was a cool-cat race car revving for a fast, fast ride.

Pete won the race just like that.

Then *SPLAT!* the race car went flat.
Now what good is a box that looks like a mat?!

The box was BIG
and it was GROOVY.
The box could be
something new.

Suddenly Pete's imagination
grew and grew and grew ...

Even though a flat box was not in the plan,

Pete imagined it was a stage

for his jammin' rock band!

Sometimes our plans just don't go right.
But it doesn't mean the day can't be OUT-OF-SIGHT!
If you use your imagination, you will see
just how GROOVY your day can be!

When you want to dream
of something new,
thinking outside the box is
the grooviest thing to do!